overl

overlove

Geraldine Snell

Dostoyevsky Wannabe Originals
An Imprint of Dostoyevsky Wannabe

First Published in 2018
by Dostoyevsky Wannabe Originals
All rights reserved
© Geraldine Snell

Dostoyevsky Wannabe Originals is an imprint of Dostoyevsky Wannabe publishing.

This is a work of fiction. The names, characters and incidents portrayed in it are the work of the author's imagination. Any resemblance to actual persons, living or dead, events or localities is entirely coincidental.

Cover design by Dostoyevsky Wannabe from an image by Geraldine Snell
dostoyevskywannabe.com

ISBN-9781726793940

No parts of this publication may be reproduced, stored in a retrieval system, or transmitted in any form or by any means, electronic, mechanical, photocopying, recording, or otherwise, without the prior written permission of the copyright owner.

This book is sold subject to the condition that it shall not, by way of trade or otherwise, be lent, resold, hired out, or otherwise circulated without the publisher's prior consent in any form of binding or cover other than that in which it is published and without a similar condition including this condition being imposed on the subsequent purchaser. Under no circumstances may any part of this book be photocopied for resale.

"Are not desire and love a sort of internal sun, the rays of which we long to receive from one another? Could not this happening create a bridge between our natural and our spiritual belongings, and so permit humanity to fulfil itself? Our tradition did not reveal the importance of such a possible event to us, except, perhaps, when it tried to approach some mystical phenomenon linked to the disclosure of a divine being. I think that desire and love between us have always a share in mystical experience and are always confronted with a negative path. How many times must we give up the illusion of a perception of the other as other before getting to be able to meet this other? How many times must we transform our bodily sensations, our feelings, our intuitions and thoughts before approaching a real sharing?"

- Luce Irigaray, via Daisy Lafarge

All of this is true★

★Except the names – I changed the names.

Geraldine Snell

Wednesday 2nd November, 23:00

The Gig: Leeds, Yorkshire

I can't remember the first time I clocked you, or even whether it was actually more a creeping awareness than a flick-of-a-switch moment, but I suppose at some point during my occasional streaming of your band's videos I must've noticed *you* – so serene, self-possessed; so sexy! – all deft limbed at the drum kit, for me to have begun imagining you looking at me, you smiling at me, you cradling me, you fucking me etc.: my hitherto benign crush goes into overdrive when I last minute decide to

attend your gig when your band comes to town… I'd say to watch you from afar but at the performance I'm stood so close: I stare at you, I take you in, I film you – but only for a few seconds, I'm not an actual weirdo – and I *swear* our eyes meet, generating bUTTERfLIES in my belly; satisfied that your flesh form has the same hold over me as your digital representation, I'm convinced – in the ole chemical rush of the lust-love sensation – that the feeling's mutual so afterwards on the train I

google you, astonished that your personal Facebook page is the top result - tentatively, I click through your profile pictures to check it's truly you before

I hover my finger over the +ADD FRIEND button – my finger trembling, retracting from and extending back towards it, hesitating – my heart rate quicKenING to the extent that I have to keep the finger still and touch my finger with the phone screen rather than the other way round. I tremble as the train glides, telling myself it's no biggie… I add people I don't know sometimes and it's cool; whilst we don't have mutual friends some of your friends are friends with some of my friends so I *ADD* you anyway. I fantasise and revel in daydreams of you, replaying the moments our eyes possibly probably definitely met in the sticky projector reel of my custard-like mind over and over and over and over until suddenly you message:

overlove

Hello..?

which I see immediately: I know you're there on the other side!! I got CHillS, they're multiplyin'... ultimate butterflies Curt, you *exist*! Your fingertips just tapped your end of the message window so we're basically tOUCHing but now what do I say??!?! Of course in my mind I imagine it seamlessly: a logistical blag-less hook-up, an impossible melding of two distinct bodies, lewd yet lofty hopes skewing my rationality... why can't you just read my mind? You see, I'm no groupie seductress! I'm a coward behind the keyboard *and* I'm on the last train back – to Mack's no less! – with an early start and a big day at work tomorrow. Various scenarios involving taxis and hotels course through my head but as well as practicalities I start to question if your "..?" – which I interpret as perhaps curious, which I *could* interpret as flirtatious – is actually a defensive "..?": a *WHO ARE YOU..? do I even know you..?*

Because maybe you're taken/partnered/betrothed maybe you're knackered maybe you're out with the band maybe you don't know or care who I am but I WondEr: do you recognise me from the gig – are you thinking "that's my brown-eyed gal, alright" – cos I wanna believe I wanna believe *oh* you call hello and your hello resounds in the empty wishing well of our chat window

and I see it, I know that you know I've seen it and time is of the essence because if I don't reply you might decline so how how how should I respond? and I WondEr: do you feel as keyed up - even in a bad way - as I? I start to type

conscious that you might be there on the other side, seeing the "..." animation, seeing how long I'm taking to formulate some REASON?! I split-second settle on a casual fellow musician vibe... I wanna know about your gear DRUMMER BOY:

23:41
Hiyaaaa. Was just at the gig and having a Google on the train about

the drum pad but can't find much so added you to say NICE ONE because it was ace but also what is your gear? Or is it a secret? Lol. I make music and really wanna try 'live-ify' it cos totally reliant on laptop at the moment

I wanna know what drum-pad you use?!?! I mean, I do but I could've trawled the nerd forums for that info… is it not clear that what I *really* want is to be yours but that I couched it in technical curiosity to test the waters, to seem cool, to gauge the tone of your response? As much as my body is high on the love juice now coursing through it, as much as my womb wanders, I know in my mind of minds I'm being daft… still, I'm a puppet on a string, Curt: I want you more than I want anything right now but somehow not enough to just say it straight, it seems. You reply:

23:46
Super simple. Look up Roland spd-sx. That's it!

and
ohhhh
that
hurts,

it's a closed response with an icy tone, although in a split-second brimming with a thousand fleeting daydreams I read "sx" as sex in the same way I fill in the gaps on license plates but NO: my soaring heart SINks but I need to keep that momentum going, this rush is too much a crutch, so I'll write and write and write…

Geraldine Snell

Thursday 3rd November, 00:30

Mack's House: Bingley, Yorkshire

Dear Curt,
Firstly, let me apologise for what to you must've seemed an out of the blue friend request. I'm not yet decided on whether I'll send you the following but I suppose you actually messaging me really caught me off guard. Yes, I don't know you, and yes, you were right to scout that out before accepting a friend request from me. Why, indeed, did I add you? It certainly wasn't to ask you about your drum pad…

The truth is, the whole evening – during which I attended your gig in Leeds and became convinced that my attraction to you was somewhat reciprocated, given the fleeting eye contact I think we maybe shared – has left me high and dry. Now I'm back from the gig, unable to sleep despite my best attempts to put it out of my mind and calm down, I've found myself with no alternative but to sit here and write to you.

How did I come to be at the gig in Leeds on this cold November day? My parents of all people – they're pretty hip – had bought tickets ages ago but I wasn't fussed about attending with them because I figured I could do what I sometimes do and watch recordings of live performances from the comfort of my bed or sofa, where I'm free to sink into the rhythms – free to get off on watching you – worlds away from the bodies which blur into one hostile mass in a live scenario; bodies exclaiming things like "this is SICK", bodies with arms outstretched filming it all, bodies blocking my 5ft2 view, bodies obscuring soft beginnings and subtle endings with obnoxious whooping and premature applause.

I'd been teaching at the art college next to the venue and had seen your tour bus at lunchtime. Well, by 'seen' I mean I perambulated said venue's perimeter with the vain hope that I'd chance upon the 'fit drummer' aka you. I think I once spotted Father John Misty having a fag on that street but in hindsight it might've just been a roadie.

Anyway, I went alone and queued from 7pm and was almost at

the very front of the stage within twenty minutes. Stood before me was a couple who could've moved half a foot to the left and freed up some space for me to lean on the barrier to the right, but they were too busy flirting and pouring whisky from a bottle in the girl's handbag into their plastic cups – too busy talking loudly over the support act's set – to notice me, probably. I was gonna go for it and stand there anyway but it worked out ok because I could see you perfectly through the soft aperture formed by their sloping shoulders and adjoined upper arms.

Being stood so close afforded me the opportunity to observe the withering looks, smirks and grimaces you exchanged on stage. That was quite thrilling to me. You see, I understood. I *understand*. I could see your fatigue, the knowing glances shared with bandmates, the way you cringed and creased up in mockery of your frontman playing to the crowd. I feel for you having to tour, to play those beats to whoops and screams night after night, and whilst I was certainly immersed in the music and attuned to the chemistry you (plural) were transmitting, I couldn't take my eyes off *you* (singular). I'm sure you looked back, but maybe it was just a glitch in your ambivalent crowd-scanning? I feel like there's something deep at play here, and if it feels so strong to me there's no way you didn't feel it too, right?

Geraldine Snell

Thursday 3rd November, 19:00

Home: Oakworth, Yorkshire

Curttttttt, this sensation is delicious! There's this heaving tingling feeling in my chest and heart and I'm soaring around with none of the ordinary physical constraints, running off it as if it's fuel with little regard for the sleep-dep or puppy love-esque single-mindedness.

But back to you:

Your position in the centre of the stage must have something to do with it; it almost reinforces that you are the source of this primal, undulating rhythm – you are keeping the beat – and I am transfixed by watching your movements as the sticks extend from your body and your feet tap the bass pedal and hi-hat so intuitively. There's something incredibly titillating about your drumming demeanour in itself, but live it was something else, particularly when I clocked you licking your lips and closing your eyes as the pace quickened and the song crescendoed into sublime noise. mmmmm.

After sleeping on it, and reviewing the short video I took of you, I really think you did make eye contact! You see, the lighting wasn't your typical gig situation where the audience are in the dark, which made it all pretty surreal because being stood so close and having these between-song moments that were relatively well lit seemed to narrow the chasm between performers and audience. I know you looked at me Curt. I know we shared a brief reciprocal gaze or ten before you sideways-averted, or I – conscious of looking stalker-ish – fixed my eyes on your sticks or kit instead. Perhaps in reality you couldn't make out faces, but I guess this whole thing so far has been me attributing significance to gestures that were only ever accidental, if they even existed at all…

overlove

Sunday 6th November, 00:40

Rose's Flat: New Cross, London

Who says our digitally mediated lives are cold and emotionless? From my perspective, those fleeting message exchanges carried a huge weight. Days have passed and I still haven't replied to your message which, admittedly, in no way invited a response. I'm at my bezzie Rose's in London and I can't exactly borrow her laptop to write you a creep-ass love letter like some 12 year old, can I Curt?

I guess it would've been weird if you'd been super friendly, but that "super simple" was a bit patronising: it sits on top of all the times a boy has said something about keeping it simple, as if anything is fuckin SIMPLE?! Maybe I invaded your personal space but HEY, it's your profile that's publically viewable from google, it's your privacy settings that permit me to message before we're friends. Some would say you're *asking for it*, public boy! You still haven't accepted or declined. Maybe if you'd just declined me none of this would've happened, but you dangled yourself in front of me with that coy, cautious "Hello..?" before crushing it all with your simple response.

Anyway, I'm beat and ready to sleep, but I formulate a simple, polite and potentially flirtatious response – depending on how much you read into these things... probably not as much as me, that's for sure! – to send you. I select a coy, blushy emoji which I feel reflects both my inner being right now and the way I feel at the thought of you. Still somewhat paralysed by the anxiety prickling from my lungs through to my fingertips, I again push my finger with the screen rather than the screen with my finger as I respond:

00:47

Thanks Curt

Sunday 6th November, 18:30

Rose's Flat: New Cross, London

So my friend Paula says there's no such thing as reverse sexual predation because women can't really be sexual predators in the same way; I suppose you just get the 'mad bitch' trope of Kathy Bates in Misery or Glenn Close boiling the bunny in Fatal Attraction. I think I agree with her but I'm still a pervert creep. Woe is me!

As a person I'm actually pretty chilled! Well, not chilled but I'm not some uptight repressed beta female, if that's what you're imagining. Whatever that is, I just did some online quizzes and I'm 70% high alpha, 44% mid beta; I am the warrior worrier, the INTJ-turbulent, the Jungian seeker, the hermit come life of the party currently plagued/graced with the mysterious libido of a teenager.

Still, I haven't acted. Half of me thinks I will send you these letters I've been writing but I'm having more fun pushing it as far as it'll go without participation from you: there's a reason we're all shouting into our own echo chambers these days, whether anyone's listening or not. Beyond the letters, you did a DJ set in Brixton last night and I'm not enough of a real stalker to have actually gone to it… in body at least - maybe you saw my coy "Thanks Curt" whilst you were there? Maybe you didn't give it a second a thought? Either way, I'm still here in the big smokey and naturally I am assuming I will bump into you at the bonfire or pub I'm headed to because that's how these things work, right? London's a small place really and I know the universe wants our bodies to be acquainted.

overlove

Monday 7th November, 17:00

Wellcome Collection: King's Cross, London

So… curt Curt,
It seems I didn't 'bump into you' in London. I'm just sat killing time before my train back up north enjoying this moment to write and reflect after a weekend chock full of gallery gallivanting and catching up with pals. I mean, overall it has been a positive and productive trip but I am still stuck-record dwelling on you; still adrift in loveish malaise. Do I need to give over with this destructive crushing, this self-perpetuated carrot on a stick scenario? Do I really want to make mountains out of molehills and experience such intense oscillations of mood and emotion? And do I even have a choice? I feel like my whole being's been hijacked by some holy force whether I like it or not…

I am trying to put myself in your shoes; to empathise with how you would feel if you knew I was writing to you in this way. I'm sorry if it's creepy. I hope you'll be flattered and curious. I hope that so much. I'm not the worst person to be adored by, am I? I think you would find me rather adorable too, Curt. I think there'd be a lot of chemistry between us because that's why I'm attracted to you; my body knows and my mind's its fool.

Geraldine Snell

Thursday 10th November, 19:10

Mack's House: Bingley, Yorkshire

Ok Curt, if I'm completely honest, I've kind of forgotten about you. In the midst of Trumpgate and me having to write an essay about learning theories, you are almost off my mind.

Well, it's not totally true. I've been listening to your band, remembering how you sang or mimed along to the new tunes at the gig last week: remembering how I stood as tall as I could, how I tried to establish eye contact, how you scanned the crowd coolly, indifferently; remembering your soft but strong features in motion; remembering your effortless, nimble hands and feet keeping those beats, your exposed shins, your tall, slender frame in that black t-shirt, the way the light played on your Jesus-like hair which flopped with the beat; remembering the polite little waves and awkward bow you did as you headed off the stage <3 God, it was so sweet how your eyes closed and your head tipped slightly upwards as you kept the rhythm so reliably, drummer boy! Maybe I haven't forgotten you at all.

You mustn't feel creeped out by these observations, by the way. I'm just an observant person, so what can I say? Of course I've been thinking of you whilst listening to the new album, paying particular attention to the drums. I don't even know if the drums on the track are you though? They're probably just midi, right? See I *was* genuinely curious when I asked about the drum pad! I do need to get my arse in gear and live-ify my songs! Maybe I'll write one about you… maybe one day you'll keep the beat for ME, Curt?

Although being back up North with Mack and thinking about some of the other guys I've crushed on recently, I know it's silly. I know in my heart that Mack's just right. I mean, he looks like the bastard lovechild of Rob Lowe and Isabella Rossellini! He's a visionary musician artiste! And the funniest, coarsest person I've ever met! And he's from the same part of the world and we both kind of call it home! And he can cook incredibly well! Jesus, he's amazing – he's probably the best person in the world! And we've been together for nearly 7 years! And we have a shared sensibility: I mean, where you wrote a dissertation on house and techno, he wrote about the commodification of lo-fi production styles to signify aura or authenticity in contemporary music! Frickin hell you're weirdly similar though, as people go.

Come to think of it, you actually have pretty much the same type of face and hairline, although his lips are plumper, the slope of your nose is straighter, his eyes are greener, your hair is long golden brown and his is short and black etc… but besides that! Sorry I hadn't mentioned him before, I thought that bringing up my life mate might thwart the possibility of our rendezvous but I suppose the fact that I've bagged this guy proves to you that I'm not a total freakazoid; that I'm not a threat?

Because he loves me enough to put up with my crushes, my theoretical insistence on polyamory even though he's sure he's a one gal guy (at least at the moment), my obsession with you. I told him I was writing to you. He just took the piss out of me and said I was nuts and that you'd be incredibly creeped out if I actually send you this.

I asked him if he thinks you'd fancy me back and he said you're a touring musician and probably get the best looking women in the world throwing themselves at you everywhere you go. He said the last thing you need is these letters to further inflate your ego. I think maybe he's just scared that you'd fall in love with me and I'd run off with you, so he's negging me to prevent that, as much as I reassure him that that's not what this is all about.

Geraldine Snell

Saturday 12th November, 02:04

Home: Oakworth, Yorkshire

Indeed, Curt, what is this all about? I'm back after a night in the pub (see, I'm sprinkling in these little details about me and my life because I do have one, I swear) and I'm feeling a bit woozy and I've just followed you on soundcloud and watched a YouTube video where your hair is short and your glasses are small and I hear your real life voice as you talk about the rainbow forming at the moment you performed Rainbows at ATP! How weird is that? You have a musical voice, a happy person's voice. You seem like a happy guy. I also watched a video of who I am guessing is your mum, and your voices are so similar: perhaps one could say you got it (your melodic intonation) from your mama!

Earlier in the week I went for a swim with Louise and told her I'd moved on to you crush-fixation wise and was writing about it, but she took it to mean that I'd actually got off with you… I then had to had to sheepishly explain that no, I added you and you messaged me, but that the rest of it's just in my head; that I'm a serious, highly functioning, professional adult human and have been actively nourishing a love infatuation with a guy in a band in my head. I guess it felt a bit silly when I said it out loud!

I just can't endure the idea that the ceaseless machinations, stuck-record ruminations and WiLd confabulations that hog my being and stave off sleep are in vain, though. Let's be real, if – as my crap attempt at an ulterior motive message, your curt response and my wimpish thanks indicates – none of this is going to result in real life romance then at least it can go somewhere in a literary sense? I suppose as long as I can pass it off as a subverting or reversal of the romantic artist dude/muse trope, a development in the expression of the female gaze, then this is more than a juvenile exercise?

Although this is no intellectual game, Curt! This is life, not art! I'm worried because were our sexes in reverse, this activity would most definitely be seen as predatory at worst and misguidedly creepy at best. Think about it: a female musician receiving a letter

overlove

of adoration from a delusional maniac who details his perception of reciprocally keen eye contact, his watching her strained facial expressions and his arousal at subsequent daydreams of sex: maybe I'm no better? Where is the line between nymph and pervert? And what's with the pathologising of hypersexuality ANYWAY? And… is this even about sex?

Inevitably I'd find you disappointing very quickly irl because how could someone ever live up to the dream Other I've constructed in my head? I recently read "The Eden Project: In Search of the Magical Other" by some Jungian therapist and it's all about how we project all our shit onto our romantic partners so we don't have to take responsibility for our own journey, for our individuation; why would you when you can 'fall in love' and seek 'home' through another? It's basically my bible at the moment, although it's still just some guy's theories about some guy's theories. Who knows what's actually occurring in us when we fall in love? Even the notion of falling implies that the whole thing's mystifying and unknown.

I really don't understand the whys and hows of my limerent longing. Of course, I know better than to think that being validated by you would actually result in satisfaction or happiness. I think I'm a just bit addicted to infatuation. I mean, it must be addictive, because there's dopamine and endorphins and stuff in the mix and that neurochemical love euphoria is akin to a crack high. It's not like teenage infatuation though, when I'd fixate on a particular blank canvas of a lad at school, desperate for him to feel the same way and to have the balls to declare it. Not that I had boyfriends at school, I was "just a speccy 4 eyed geek" as the objet d'amour of my primary school years' best friend once termed me in front of him. Maybe now I do have a choice about whom I'm obsessed with? Even so, I choose you! And maybe the guy I pass on my walk for my morning train to Leeds sometimes, but he's only a fleeting fancy; his eye contact is too keen and reciprocal for me to actually long for his adoration and validation.

But anyway, back to the YouTube rabbit hole I've entered, I'm now watching you talk about a Mozart piece you're about to play on a grand piano. You awkwardly introduce it, saying how it's unconventional because there are bits here and bits there and you heighten the stool a little, also awkwardly, because you're tall. Now you're playing and it's special because it's *you*; the notes are resonating even if you're a little staccato, a little clunky. How do you feel about me criticising you, Curt? Do you feel like it's totally unwarranted or do you like that I'm a lady that says it how it is?

overlove

Saturday 12th November, 21:30

Home: Oakworth, Yorkshire

Curt, I'm officially bored now. In all my lugubrious logging of lingering thoughts of you, in all my indulging in idyllic imaginings of us, living's taken a bit of a back seat. Of course, daily life is marching on. I'm not paralysed by my pining or anything. It's just always there – hovering, agitating – in the middle-ground of my mind; something to focus on through the drudgery of winter amidst the adult pressures weighing down on me.

In the evenings I'm tired and listless with assignments and art to procrastinate from, so I while away most getting just a little bit high on a single skin joint out of the attic window of my parent's house before floating down content streams, fishing for something which I seem to have found, at least partially, in my obsession with you. I'm horny for all sorts of impossible things, horny in a sad and lonely way despite being sexually and romantically satisfied in what is basically as perfect a relationship as can be.

Poor little me, eh? I don't think I'm the only one, judging by the proliferation of memes and social media activity that's pervaded by a typically privileged, needs-met, first-world-problems flavour of boredom and malaise, which is then somewhat offset by the sense of community – the "what a time to be alive"-ness – obtained from scrolling down those infinite feeds in search of something that makes the pleasure signals ping.

I think it's what the theorist Mark Fisher termed *depressive hedonia*: "an inability to do anything but pursue pleasure... There is a sense that 'something is missing' – but no appreciation that this mysterious, missing enjoyment can only be accessed beyond the pleasure principle". There I go, referencing cultural theory to excuse by way of articulating the vices that I – and probably most of us – grapple with in this climate of excess. I think there's something to be said for naming and theorising; whilst it rarely actually changes or improves us or the world it's a form of distancing that offers some respite for the intellectually inclined.

Anyway: I don't really *need* visual assistance when masturbating, certainly the visions I produce in my mind surpass anything I can watch on a screen, but increasingly I'm preferring to watch something to get me going, even if it's just because the option's there. As I've said, I've been watching you on YouTube, but I'm just not satisfied by the snippets I see! As the drummer the camera never lingers on you long enough and you're out of focus and marginal in the one interview I can find you in. Your form is not peripheral to me, Curt, so I decide to capture a longer shot of you from a live take music video for another band you drum for, which I can slow down and play on a loop whilst I work on myself. There are glimmers of you sipping a glass of water at 03:27, laughing at 03:38, bringing the beat back in at 04:00 – your body jerking and head nodding as you drum – and creasing up at 04:46 at what I presume is the irrepressible joy induced by the horn section.

It's after the 6-minute mark that the perfect segment presents itself. At 06:23, it really hones in on you bouncing gently on your stool before the camera cuts away, returning to linger on you for a solid ten seconds at 06:31 which – slowed down to a quarter of the speed – reveals what you must look like during sex.

Your mouth is slightly open, your brow furrowed in concentration, you lick your lips and close your eyes which, at one point, look slightly crossed as if your front brain has clicked off and you're being driven by entirely animal impulses, and I imagine you thrusting slowly into me as I apply a firm but gentle motion to my clit with the middle and ring finger of my right hand, the left penetrating my almost achingly empty, yielding and incredibly wet hole in imitation of your dick, and I increase the vigour and speed – still watching your sex-like movements on the screen, still imagining your eyes on me, your arms round me, your hands on me, your dick in me – in the quick build up to a first orgasm which is over before I can moan "Oh Curt"!

I come back to myself, beginning to sense the absurdity and creepiness of what I'm doing, but decide it needn't end yet; there's no point going to all that trouble for one orgasm, so I go

overlove

back for a second, third, fourth, fifth and sixth because they're coming particularly thick and fast given the stimuli. After a particularly long and hollow post-come ceiling stare, I tap the spacebar to pause the looped video with my left thumb – which escaped the action unscathed – and scuttle into my freezing, dark bathroom to rinse off and brush my teeth before attempting to sleep the rest of the evening away.

Tuesday 15th November, 15:00

Mack's House: Bingley, Yorkshire

Still thinking about Curt but only in order to move writing on.

overlove

Friday 25th November, 18:30

Home: Oakworth, Yorkshire

I haven't thought about it at all really, I swear, although I know you are DJing in London tomorrow. I had half a mind to bez down on the coach and come and watch you, or even offer to sit on the door as you advertised publicly on your Facebook page (which you have not friended or declined me on but which I'm nonetheless checking semi-regularly; I see posts that are set to 'Public', obviously.)

I just watched a live video performance on Letterman and your drums hadn't arrived and you were playing a minimal set up and looking real cute with shorter hair and glasses. You looked nerdier then, you look sexier now. I like it! But I liked it before too. The way Letterman pointed at you patronisingly and asked you questions but didn't wait for your answers really pissed me the fuck off, as an American might say. I would've had your back Curt.

I feel so frazzled and fatigued. Fatiguedly frazzled. Frazzledly fatigued. The world is becoming a little too heavy again, and Mack's in Tokyo and I miss him like hell. It's weird that in the previous entry I wrote about you in third person rather than addressing YOU. I mean, am I addressing you or am I just writing about *it*? Who even are *you*?

Sunday 27th November, 01:34

Home: Oakworth, Yorkshire

You are Curt, vigilant Curt, on Facebook, testing the waters with your cautious "Hello..?" You are goofy with a hole in your crotch on KEXP, hero Curt mitigating your singer's timing blob on the last song. You are Curt Hertz on the decks. But in my mind you are always Drummer Boy, keeping the beat while I drift along.

Geraldine Snell

Sunday 1st January, 17:00

Home: Oakworth, Yorkshire

Well look what day it is… happy New Year, Curt! Whatever that means? It seems Christmas and co. came and went in the usual whirlwind. I was flying at a million miles an hour before the hols began and I dropped like Wile E. Coyote drops off the cliff in Looney Toons; a spectacular fall from my previous state of too-good-to-be-true hyper-grace which peaked – or troughed, I suppose – during an acute anguish sesh, triggered by that damned empty sick grief sensation that's been present but dormant for a little too long, and consisted of 3 hours of hysterical sobbing in my room in the dark after Christmas dinner.

Yep, I plummeted way beyond the point where my fool's paradise can tide me over or buoy me up. In fact, I think it went the other way: this bittersweet head-trip's had me coasting at a cost. Although the crimbo deluge was followed on Boxing Day by the onset of my period after a 39 day cycle!!! I think there's something in my theory that the longer or more irregular the cycle, the worse the mood and other symptoms are, not that the docs give a shit.

It seems I've been asleep at the wheel, and to a degree, thoughts of you have been my cruise control. Ha, I hope you appreciate the driving metaphors Curt, I'm cringing and punching the air with self-satisfaction in equal measure at my clichéd punning. I guess this letter's a little thank you: for existing; for being handsome but also in my league enough for a possible encounter not to be a total pipe-dream; for being mysterious and elusive enough to allow me this space to monologue.

I had a thought about this writing, and surely you can't object if I publish it one day, particularly if I anonymise you? It's not like I'm slandering you or anything, I mean, I know I said I know you but I know that I don't know you know you, and the reader'll know that, right? I think the only thing I'm guilty of here is being a self-sabotaging creep, actually: of lusting loving longing as depression diversion and anxiety management, a

overlove

strategy for being, albeit a shit one.

Friday 6th January, 08:40

K7 Bus: Oakworth, Yorkshire

No, as conclusive as that last one sounded, it's not over yet: I've got too mundane an immediate future to not heighten life to art. Sorry not sorry.

overlove

Sunday 8th January, 00:50

Home: Oakworth, Yorkshire

I'm vile. Although I did write the beginnings of some poignant lyrics which were – like this writing – initially inspired by you (like, not you in particular, but this projected ideal of you as this magical Other that if I connected with romantically it would complete me and I would feel whole rather than a lone, individual in my own head with no proper, solid 100% same page connections to anyone ever because that is impossible because we are human). The melody and chords are beautiful as well but I need to sort the end of the chorus and write a verse so don't judge prematurely!! It goes:

Bridge:
I watch you from afar, you're on my radar,
But it's all in my head, not a word has been said,
But when your eyes meet mine, the feeling is so divine,
How I revel in the rush, that sensation I can't trust

Chorus:
I… ma-a-a-ake, the sa-a-a-a-ame, mista-a-a-a-ake
I….fa-a-a-all, from gra-a-a-a-ace, agai-ai-ai-ai-ain
Can't… ta-a-a-ake, the wei-ei-ei-ei-eight, this sta-a-a-a-ate.
No… lo-o-o-ove, It's al-al-all too much, I can't contain the rush??
(IMPROVE)!

Geraldine Snell

Friday 13th January, 19:45

Home: Oakworth, Yorkshire

A few things have reminded me of you today Curt, funnily enough. Firstly, one of my students was describing how she has fully stalked this American or Canadian woman whose home videos she found on YouTube and has basically got a full picture of her life, googling other family members that appear in the home videos in order to compile a full family tree that goes six generations back. The way she talked about this old lady Erna on the other side of the world was so affectionate. A different student has created a character based on a childhood imaginary friend devised with her sister.

It made me feel not so strange for doing what I'm doing with you; there are many precedents for this kind of activity in the expanded field of art. I tell myself that this legitimises it but perhaps this is tired ground?

Either way my searching skills – honed through years of library labouring – together with my possibly presumptuous powers of deduction have led me to the conclusion that the Leela that made your graphic is perhaps your life mate: the first time you appear on her Instagram is mid-March 2016 and your presence in the image feed indicates more than platonic paldom. Image location tags also give away what may be your dwelling place but when I google that it conflicts with the electoral roll postcode given for you at 123.com! Worry not though: I'm not sad or mad enough to pay for 'full access' in order to loiter near your door, particularly when you appear to have a girlfriend anyway. When I'd got over this bubble-bursting reality bite – which wasn't too painful as I'm an expert builder/mourner of frangible love illusions – I was excited to see that her areas of interest include mental health and the female gaze!!!!

I mean, if you've got a gf that savvy then you shouldn't be freaked out by this, and neither should she! Because what I'm doing here is being a mentally ill female subjecting you to my volatile female gaze, with all the complexity and power dynamics that involves! Maybe you can both laugh about it anyway, or

overlove

maybe you fancy a threesome? I've never done that before but there's a first for everything.

I think you two are chilled. From what I can surmise from your post about going East and her Instagram post tagged in Goa, you're in India having a ball. That's so nice. I am happy for you, even if it shatters my illusion about my capacity to 'save' you, sweep you off your feet, or be validated and completed by your falling for me. But I'm beyond that idea of love anyway now, because it's daft.

Geraldine Snell

Friday 13th January, 23:00

Home: Oakworth, Yorkshire

Hi again Curt,

It's 11pm now and it was a tiring day to end an exhausting week. It's also Friday 13th, which is of no relevance here. I'm just trying to paint a picture for you Curt, of me sat here in me birthday suit, eyes red raw but finally relishing this moment to record and reflect. Yes, I'm naked but not in *that* way, as the recently deceased John Berger would say: naked as opposed to nude.

I saw an advert today which featured – as a model – the first guy I crushed on after getting with Mack! Incidentally, he was a drummer too. It's strange but comforting how things converge and make sense, or at least resonate across time and place, within life's chaos.

Back then at the tender age of 18 I was recovering from a moderately severe depressive episode by retreating into a spectacular diamond-rainbow-starshine-blossom-lined gold and chocolate gilded cocoon come Garden of Eden in my relationship with Mack, putting my remaining focus into my art Foundation course. Then this guy swaggered into the studio with his long hair and tattoos and I – newly monogamous, overwhelmed with art and adult-life angst, living an ascetic friendless hermit lifestyle, covered in cystic acne from the Dianette the docs gave me to improve what had hitherto been merely moderate – found his nonchalance a little too irresistible.

I doubt he ever noticed but there was a tender moment when he came and sat next to me on his laptop whilst I read T.S. Eliot's Waste Land aloud on a bench in the corridor as part of some wanky performance – which I was cunningly using as a way to escape formal art discourse through reading literature – and we talked about his tolerance break from weed and the subtle insidiousness of the stuff. In hindsight, maybe he was just there for better Wi-Fi.

That caused bad juju between me and Mack at the time, because how could I love *him* if I wanted someone else? How

overlove

naïve we were about our myriad propensities for love.

Geraldine Snell

Tuesday 17th January, 07:50

Home: Oakworth, Yorkshire

I had my first dream about you last night, Curt. It's the first that I remember anyway, although I don't remember much of it now.

overlove

Friday 3rd February, 23:30

Home: Oakworth, Yorkshire

Hi Curt. The florid language used in your social media postings suggests a poetic sensibility and splendid degree of linguistic refinement. Maybe you will appreciate this literary experiment of mine, at least on formal grounds? You are living it up in London with Leela and pals but also feeling the weight of world, feeling compelled to protest the shit that's going down with Trump, you wear singlets, you drum, you party, you seek alternative news sources, you eXiSt!! <3 x x x

Geraldine Snell

Tuesday 14th February, 20:30

Home: Oakworth, Yorkshire

I came on here to recap a dream I had last night, and only as I've typed the date have I realised it's Valentine's Day! So Happy Valentine's Day Curt! I am full of cold, fatigued again (but without the frazzled) and a little heavy from Mark Fisher's memorial, which I attended at Goldsmiths the other day with Rose. Yeah, the Mark Fisher I mentioned earlier re: depressive hedonia – who hit so many nails on the head with his piercing way of addressing the nitty-gritty of culture, consumption and existence under late capitalism – was defeated by his black dog last month. It has both awakened me to the reality of depression and suicide at a time when I'm struggling to keep such thoughts at bay and piqued my concern for our broader socio-political situation, as relatively privileged as I am within it.

One of my tutors has advised me to 'save my spoons' because I'm burnt-out, iron deficient and up and down like a yo-yo moods-wise. I suppose that means saving my energy for the zillion assignments, reflections and files I have to keep on top of teaching, and not getting carried away falling in love with people that don't exist and expending vital life fuel writing about it.

But that's no fun, is it Curt?

How and why describe a dream to someone who wasn't in it? I've always wondered about dream telepathy though, for example if your brain invents a face that you meet in your dream, is that a real person who is also dreaming somewhere about meeting you? Of course, you're not an invented person though. Even so, I'd like to think you were dreaming the same thing at the same time, wherever you were last night, whether you knew it was me or not.

The dream consisted of me driving round and bumping into other cars on a strange dream island where your band came to play and stay. Far from being a blissful reverie where we carelessly cavorted, you still had this distanced aloofness which made me pine for you upon waking. At one point I was walking alone along a precarious pebble path on a cliff edge in order to scale down a safer slope to a hot spring by the beach where I intuitively knew you were close by, horsing around with pals. I reached the spring and found a shallow pool, steam dissipating from its glimmering teal surface, where my sudding up my naked body seemed to catch your attention.

You came to me and lifted me like a child, fondling my soapy flesh with the spring's magical water, swirled with softening oils and the scent of lemongrass and balmy pine. I felt warm and cocooned, as if mum had just lifted me out of the bath and into a warm towel: you attended to me, not in a sexual way, but sensuously, carefully, erotically; you somehow held me in your arms whilst you soothed and massaged my shoulders, thighs, boobs and bum as my body stiffened and loosened under your hold, and whilst you were visibly somewhat stirred, the subtle hunger detectable in your eyes was as cool and serene as your demeanour at the gig, and you soon put me down before disappearing off out of sight, leaving me alone in the water, its soft current rinsing the fragrant suds off my body and sending them downstream.

Geraldine Snell

Sunday 19th February, 10:20

Mack's House: Bingley, Yorkshire

Well Curt, it looks like you are becoming a frequent figure in vivid dreams of late. I had another last night, after researching Venice Biennale with the intention of visiting this summer, and looking on Leela's Facebook to sneak a peek at some recently uploaded pictures of your crew in India! Maybe they weren't meant to be viewable by the 'Public', but they were: I showed Mack and he was pretty smug about the beach shot and being in better shape than you, as if that's what this is about!!! I let him have his little victory, though.

Two of your friends from the India pictures are actually mutual friends with the two poshest people I know! I don't mean toff-posh, but cultural capital cosmopolitan London upbringing posh. I guess I only mention that because however Keighley comprehensive my origins, it strikes me that we're part of a privileged, cultured elite that – from my experience – often critiques things at arm's length, challenging the general idea of power and privilege but rarely how our circumstances and education afford us even the leisure and voice to do so.

Not to scrutinise your or my specific case; we all know that the privately-educated elite dominate the professions and the establishment, but there are problematic relationships between class and success in cultural professions that aren't often broached. There was a really CUTE headline today about how Tom Hiddleston played Eddie Redmayne's elephant in a school play when they were young! How cute is that? So cute that they both went to Eton and were in majorly slick productions of plays since a very a young age and acting was nurtured in them and then they chose to go into that rather than being at the top rung as Prime Minister, Army General, banker, barrister. How cute that they made a killing acting when they probably don't even need money to survive with all that inherited wealth. HOW FUCKIN CUTE EH!?!?!?!

Sorry, I digress. It's just that the personal is political; there is no such thing as the individual, as individual success. I wouldn't be

overlove

so angry if it were acknowledged, but still the myth of individual genius, of Tom Hiddleston being somehow the best actor – rather than him being a well-connected member of a social and cultural elite who has had high roles handed to him on a plate – pervades.

Anyway, that was a very convoluted roundabout way of getting onto last night's dream, the missing link being that my very awareness of Venice Biennale signifies my cultural capital, and the dream likely took place in Venice due to my researching it. I obviously felt I had to get all that off my chest before indulging in more decadent dream recall…

I dreamed of you again last night. I dreamed I went to Venice, or a dream version of Venice, with my family and you were staying in the next room with two ladies, one of which was your Leela but a dream version. I suppose you were you, but a dream version too? It was a dizzying experience and in the midst of it, it was real. I couldn't believe that of all the people that could've been staying in the room next to me, in the same hotel, in the same CITY, at the same time, it was YOU, Curt.

The room I was in was long with a low ceiling and bright with off-white light, the wall between our rooms composed of glass panels and an opaque beige blind on your side of the glass – that was sometimes raised a little, offering me a glimpse into your space – which maintained the privacy.

Being a dream I can't be sure of the order of events, and maybe I'm confabulating wildly as the day trudges on, but I distinctly remember ascending the hotel's wide, gently inclining marble staircase and catching sight of you through an ornate gilded archway, emerging from your door into the space between our rooms and the stairwell, and you were coming my way and we approached the archway at the same speed and we were the same distance from it and you didn't see me until we were about to collide and you looked up, making brief eye contact, and curtly cutely let me through and I – in the intensity of the situation, scuttling like a wounded spider – sloped hastily into my room where I slammed the door behind me, caught my breath, and peered through the spy hole, catching a glimpse of you through the archway coolly descending the stairs, eyes cast downwards, presumably indifferent to our brief encounter.

The following dream day when the sky was an eerie lilac hue which could've hinted that it was 9pm getting dark or 3am getting light – in any case, it was dream o'clock and the *feeling* was that it didn't matter – I followed some lone wanderer impulse to lonely wander outdoors, out through the hotel's veranda and onto a large lush grassy area – the kind of which I imagine you'd never find irl in stony, crumbly Venezia – all mauve in the near-dark, to find you. You know when you *know* someone you're drawn to is somewhere nearby, or you wander in order to come upon them because wandering, in transit in pursuit, is almost always preferable to being still being settled somewhere having to find some other occupation? That's what I was doing (that's what I do). And you were there with your two ladies, carefree on the veranda, at ease in the cool night air, whilst I watched from afar, perched awkwardly on the grassy mound, gazing and averting, wondering what time of night it was.

overlove

Sunday 26th February, 01:50

Home: Oakworth, Yorkshire

Hello Leela,

It'll get silly if I start writing to you, but as it happens, in a totally non ulterior motive way, I truly, madly, deeply love your illustrations. I would buy a tarot deck that you made. I would pay you to create some illustrations for this writing as a form of remuneration and olive-branch offering for any distress I may cause through my home-wrecking hussydom.

Maybe the universe brought us together for this artistic meeting of minds? Maybe the last thing you'd want is to collaborate with someone who wants to fuck your boyfriend (if he is your boyfriend, I'm totally presuming a lot of things here…) and has used him to write this pathetic, albeit epic, diary love letter, but from my perspective, good things could come of this!

Love and apologies, from woman to woman,
Geri

Curt,

I just started really resenting myself for spending time indulging in all this quasi-boy stuff rather than just getting on with making my own sick music or art, but then I thought of how my stalking you has led me to Leela's illustrations and the feminist academic I assume is your mama; how this may yet result in female empowerment and sorority!

If that sounds like I know a lot about you, it's only that which is googleable and visible on social media; if nothing else, this activity is a demonstration of how much you can piece someone together from fragments.

I've found some more fragments which have simultaneously whet my appetite for seeing you again in the flesh and put me off it due to a fear that it might be all laddy, macho, guys on the decks. Nah, there are only snippets of those vibes which inevitably come with the sight of multiple male bodies nodding, looking serious and backslapping behind a DJ booth. How I wish I was the recipient of your cool man gaze, as much as I know better.

I watch you on a phone video that someone has uploaded, your headphones pushing your hair back behind your ear; you are très elegante twizzling nobs in the red light, serene as per when you run your hands through your hair. Your body jerks and I picture fucking you and wonder: should I come to the night in March or would you recognise my face from the friend request and be creeped out?

overlove

Tuesday 7th March, 20:30

Mack's House: Bingley, Yorkshire

I think one of the reasons I keep re-thinking about you is because I listen to your band a lot, and even if you don't play the drums in the album tracks, my connection with you is still irrevocably associated with that sensual music. Plus, every day that I teach at college I see the venue where it all began.

You are doing a DJ set in London next Saturday night. You are beaming and the descriptions on your promo page are very inviting. I think I will have to come, if not to this particular event, another soon. I can gain some closure this way. I can re-see you in a smaller, more intimate context, and 'watch you from afar' as my lyrics go, in order to push this nonsense to its logical conclusion: stalking with the possible intention of casually seducing and writing up whatever unfolds.

I am conscious that you may recognise me from when I added you on Facebook five months ago, but I doubt you looked much at my photos as you didn't know who I was, and I doubt you gave me a second thought. Although you never did decline my friend request; it is still hovering *in cyberspace.*

I've gotta do it. I asked Mack and he said he can't know how he feels about it until I do. From my perspective, I can't write or fabricate a new encounter unless I actually see you. This stuff is so bound up with my real life thoughts and feelings, my integrity won't let it descend into fiction. Mack says there's this thing called artistic license, and he thinks I wouldn't come and see you unless I had seedy intentions. I told him that I think Leela will be there, and that you wouldn't fancy me anyway, and that I might not fancy you in person. I'm sure I'd be too paralysed to act or talk in the flesh, after all this fuss and build up. But I suppose we'll see? I'll see whether I can get a girlfriend to come with me – as opposed to lone me stalking strangely – so if all else fails, we will have had a laugh and a dance.

Geraldine Snell

Wednesday 15th March, 18:30

Home: Oakworth, Yorkshire

I message Rana to ask if she's down with my crazy schemes, which she is, but not this time:

18:29
In theory Rana, would you accompany me / be wing woman in low key stalking of that drummer at a night he djs at in Hackney? It's for poignant writing/art (LOL)

Hahhahaha that sounds amazing. I'd love to. What's the date??

well there's one this Saturday that i've been dithering about but i think it's too late. but there'll be another lol. unless you're free and i should totally just do it.
but there'll be another

his dj name is fuckin… curt hertz
is it wrong that that turns me on?

Ive got a refugee fundraiser gig this Saturday!
Definitely not wrong

overlove

Thursday 16th March, 22:20

Home: Oakworth, Yorkshire

Oh Curt. Leela is back in London n ur beaming this sat n ur social media postings make it so tempting but I'm knackered from teaching and studying n feeling too much n Rana's at a refugee fundraiser anyway and Rose's back up north for various real life reasons and naturally it's made me feel very silly about the whole thing; some people have real problems... But next time will be the time I watch you from afar and attempt to converse with you, to establish contact which acknowledges my creepy behaviour n goes some way toward getting Leela to create some illustrations OR getting you in bed. Peace and love x

Saturday 25th March, 19:30

Settle-Carlisle Railway: Dent, Cumbria

I'm on the train back from Edinburgh attempting to read over some of this writing but I can't take my eyes off the sublime fuchsia sunset. It's too much; I can't fathom how the other people on the train aren't even looking at it?!

I felt like a true 'sexy lady' this weekend, returning to my art school to contribute a video to a symposium aptly titled "This can only be thought of as a monologue within a dialogue", at which I saw a tutor I'd had a huge crush on outside the lecture theatre. I'd forgotten how intense his eye contact was and how much I enjoy hearing his soft Scottish accent say my name.

It's certainly good to know my attachment to you hasn't precluded other such fancies, as well given the desire I developed for a fellow symposium attendee after he and I talked about art, depression and meditating.I almost messaged him inviting him to 'meditate' together after going out with Charlotte and Chloe, when I drunkenly sped-walked 40 minutes across the city alone at 1am but something stopped me, as usual: probably the fact that I already have a soulmate and there's no such thing as light, carefree cavorting irl?

I miss you Curt.

overlove

Monday 3rd April, 18:00

Home: Oakworth, Yorkshire

So what's new Curt? I saw this guy on the train that I've seen in the pub a few times and on Tinder (which I'm only really on to window shop and research, really) and our eyes met quite intensely and his name's Curt too and when he broke eye contact it was downwards rather than sideways which is a sign of submission apparently it said so on a YouTube video about the body language of attraction and I'm thinking he looks like a bit of a bimbo or normalo but maybe I could use him as practice or have a bit of fun with him in the meantime and test out my methods of seduction on someone new just in case it happens with you one day?

Geraldine Snell

Sunday 9th April, 19:25

Home: Oakworth, Yorkshire

So I don't know if it was about transference of neurotic obsession focus away from you or just another string to add to my master-procrastinator bow – I have two teaching files and four essays to be on with this Easter – but I joined OkCupid. It's been an illuminating few days in which I realised the extent of my deluded pursuit and my misplaced energies.

As a young and – according to an OkCupidder called Guy from Israel – "conventionally attractive woman" seeking 'compartmentalised connections', naturally I received lots of creepy messages. I think I made a big mistake calling myself 'audrey_horny' and I can't change it for 30 days, but I did get talking to a cutey from Bristol and before long it descended – or ascended, depending on your disposition – into a sext. We even talked about meeting in the middle somewhere for a steamy sesh. I followed up on Friday, and didn't receive a reply on Saturday *or* Sunday! I've been tearing my hair out, refreshing the page even though if he messaged it would show. I'm so pissed off at myself for being left high and dry by some internet fuccboi with deep brown eyes and floppy black hair. I really just wanted to get some work done and I mostly have, but I'm still engaged in this frickin futile search for something I can't define?! I'm obsessed, infatuated with another guy I don't even know. He showed a bit of intimacy, validation, that he 'wanted' me and I just latched on. Now I'm thinking about looking you up or finding someone else to fixate on just to put the energy somewhere. I think it's here to stay and I need a more wholesome vent, rather than all this leaky jar hedonism.

Do you know Socrates' leaky jar analogy? I bet you're a hedonist Curt; if you like to party and are into house and techno then you must be because you need uppers to feel uninhibited and boosted enough to dance the night away, from my experience, and uppers are hedonistic and moreish.

Well the idea is, if you've got addictive or over-indulgent hedonistic tendencies, you have the constitution of a leaky jar.

overlove

You fill and fill and fill with pleasure or sensation or whatever the hell it is, but you're never full because the jar's always leaking. Maybe there's a reason humans need temperance, restraint, monogamy, asceticism, King and country, 'family values'; a life dedicated to the pursuit of fleeting pleasure is a fool's life. Although from a social control perspective, civilisation couldn't function if everyone just served their own needs. Why would people adhere to daft customs and moral edicts if they trusted and acted responsibly – consensually, of course – on their unrepressed impulses and appetites? It'd be a world of empowered, loosey goosey super people, comfortable in their own skin and sexuality, and for them lot in control – not that they're a singular entity, but… you know – it'd be fuckin chaos!

Geraldine Snell

Evening

Later on, I am messaging Mack:

 22:22

u ok then
i got nowt to update with tbh

> *yeah i'm ok... feelin a bit bummed. idk.*
> *it's like... i'm seeking a connection that doesn't exist.*
> *but i wanna seek it anyway.*

serves u right haha
fr00t l00p

> 😊

😊

> *you don't understand*
> *we're all completely alone*

👎

> *n can never connect*
> *really*

😮

lies
damn lies

> *it's true! like you. we've never REALLY connected*
> *it's just an illusion*
> *you're always in your own head*
> *you never even look me in the eye*
> *for long*

fai
l

> *there was glimmers of it when we first met.*
> *when we gazed across the bed at*
> *eachother*
> *you fuka*
> *you don't even talk to me properly about this stuff*

overlove

                    cos you take it personally
            you didn't even read the eden project

mehehehe
lighten up

                                  no
                            i feel lonely

shit son
i need to go brush ma teeth n get off here
sorry I cant reassure u via keyboard

☺

ull be fine tho

                                    ffs

come on mannnnnnne
wat

                            piss off then

fuck sake

                           all i'm sayin is
                            it's not enough
                             weltschmerz

k

        reality isn't enough. we never really connect properly
that's pretty abstract tho

                                no it's not
                         we cuddle in bed, we kiss

i mean u could say that about owt
'never enough' etc
        you only connect with me properly intimately when you're horny.
                      you n your fuckhead man brain

bollocksssss m8
point is, its pretty fuckin good
bet it's 50x better than what 99% get

                                  maybe so
                                      but
                                  it's like
                     we can't even really talk
           you say what you say, i say what i say
 you listen more to what you say, getting your own point across, over

Geraldine Snell

                    what i say
         i don't mean 'you', i just mean anyone, any 'other'

yh
i think ur overthinkin
it's not 'perfect'
but we have a nice time n a good life

                            lol
                pretty house pretty garden

😮

guess i aint gnna reach ya
ur feelin a bit EMO

                cmon you know what i mean
                    'nice time n a good life'
                            woop

geri edge-meister

            ok you brush your teeth n sleep well
            n i'll just lie here in existential crisis
                      heartbreak agony

hahhaa
u gotta see the funny side of what u just wrote

come on 🙂
   I MAAA-AAAKE THE SAAA-AA-AA-AA-AME MISTA-
                          AA-A-AA-AA-AKE
                          ye i know eegit

u pissed
bet u blazed
summat screwed ur head up

                    i had a tiny bit o weed
                          n sum booze after

lol

                            but i'm ok
                            just sad

kk well u'll be better before ya kno it

🙂

                                ye ye

overlove

                                        smug

ye
im tryin to be nice
                            ye but you're simpler than me
yh
                      anyway, go to bed. i'll turn this off too.
                    n read see how ck structures and tenses in ild.
                    a woman that sympathises with my distress
yh good idea
                                  unlike simple boy ye
love u bab speak tomorro
dw
                                            love you
ull pull thru
                                                :@

loveu crazy angel

Geraldine Snell

Tuesday 25th April, 22:10

Home: Oakworth, Yorkshire

I have just found myself simultaneously trawling through the chaff on okcupid, cyberstalking the Bristol cutey and listening to your mix on soundcloud. I guess tonight's a lonely night; it's my first night sans Mack for a few nights. I've been reading the Ethical Slut: A Practical Guide to Polyamory, Open Relationships & Other Adventures and am keen to get on with some of this stuff. I actually right-swiped a guy during my indifferent Tinder left-swiping because he was a drummer called Curt and I thought that had too much potential to pass up on, but when we matched I didn't really fancy him or have any inclination to meet him just because he was a drummer called Curt.

Anyway I'm saving myself and any extra-relationship activity for when I come and shake my booty at one of your nights, when I'll disguise myself as a carefree, sassy young thang, give you the eyes and try and engage you in flirtatious conversation, hopefully. Then you won't think I'm some kind of cyberstalking fan girl (although, what's so wrong with that?) and you'll be taken by my sextastic presence and entranced by my sexy body and enthralled by my sexy brain. That's the plan…

overlove

Monday 1st May, 18:50

Mack's House: Bingley, Yorkshire

Upon my distant and very half-arsed stalking of you I have come across a poster advertising 'inner u' – a warehouse party which encourages dancing and self-expression as socially transformative – on Leela's Instagram! It sounds like my cup of tea, and is handily located 5 minutes' walk from Rana's on the street parallel to Rose's studio, so feasibly they could've already heard about it ont'scene. Still, I feel like a country bumpkin phoney impostor, that 'someone like me' shouldn't be going to such parties, as inclusive as the descriptions sound.

It's in a few weeks and I imagine you will be there, and I need a trip down to London anyway...

I'm just thinking maybe it is a way to kill three birds with one stone: low-key stalk you, catch up and party with my pals AND discover my 'true me'? Maybe I can really think about how I 'present' myself in a setting where I will totally fully be accepted, in an environment "founded on the principle of the club space as a house for self-expression". Come to think of it, who the fuck am I? I don't really buy the idea that you can find that out on the dancefloor – for all the fleeting euphoria these things usually make me feel deeply lonely – but it's worth a shot, *right?*

Mack has given me permission to play it by ear etc. Oo, no, he just read that over my shoulder and he says I have to clarify that actually :S - he says he can't stop me, which is an entirely different thing because it's not explicit permission, and suggests a reluctant setting free in order to get me back, like a bird in a cage. His vision of paradise comes from the original Persian, meaning 'walled garden', the perfect cocoon; I keep teasing him about the fact that all I want to do is install a cat flap... is that really so wrong?

Geraldine Snell

Tuesday 9th May, 20:15

Home: Oakworth, Yorkshire

how did we get 2 here...!
join us for inner u 5: same space, same rules, but for this event we will be exploring DIY identities - we want to see u construct a persona for urself, taking inspiration from and making use of everyday objects and materials. channel ur true u...creatively :)
we are a generous and welcoming party, accountable and aware of how our actions may affect others in a space. if someone is making u feel uncomfortable during the night let one of us on the door or behind the decks know - we promise to listen and put a stop to it immediately.
there is no guestlist: everyone is equal at inner u.
see u soon! Xxx

^^^^^^ so I've booked the coach!

To London

To find my true me

Rana will come

Maybe other pals will come

And we will party

Shit can't believe it's actually happening and he's actually gonna be there and I'm gonna watch him from afar again

Shit

Shit

Shit

Shit

Him? You! YOU CURT, YOU!!!!!

But what if I make you feel uncomfortable and you let someone behind the decks know and they put a stop to it immediately and I am publicly humiliated?

What if they don't let me in because of my evil intentions?

Hehe

I just don't care anymore, I'm beyond shame. I just need to round this off! In fact, I'm so beyond myself that I don't even find 'inner u' cringey, as I'm sure my old cynical self usually would. All I knows is I got a ticket to Curtville and I hope it's one way... I've had my verse lyrics now for a while which I

overlove

could serenade you with:

It's losing its appeal, since I, fell aslee-eep at the wheel,
Gone beyo-ond right and wro-ong, I'm just looking for a way to carry on,
Cos this road winds on and o-on, if you keep the beat then I will drift along,
Never questioning the wh-hy, of, my, self-perpetuated hypomanic high

But then it goes into the "I watch you from afar..." bit and chorus, which I still haven't doctored the lyrics for. The thing I'm most stuck with though, drummer boy? The drums...

Geraldine Snell

Thursday 11th May, 17:00

Mack's House: Bingley, Yorkshire

I had a revelation whilst lying awake facing my dear dear sleeping Macky. It was a most tender moment, our foreheads and knees touching, warmth and whatever else lifting my heart as I held his slim furry thigh. I'd seen a very tender post and caption about you on Leela's Instagram, and had this overwhelming feeling of happiness and expansiveness; that you are to her what Mack is to me. That is so precious. It almost made me feel like scrapping my plan to attend the party but I've booked now and really fancy a trip to London and a dance anyway.

At that moment, as my magical Other snoozed, I got it into my head that Mack should come to inner u with me. It would be perfect! It would be balanced and sensible and would stop me having this anticipation and desperation for something to come of it. It'd be so deeply sad for us to not share it, and I will be less threatening to you because there won't be the same weird psycho lady stalker dynamic. Although I don't think he'll want to, mostly because of the blag associated with going down to London and the ball ache of staying up late partying and upsetting the body clock rather than any dramatic moralistic objection.

overlove

Tuesday 16th May, 20:30

Home: Oakworth, Yorkshire

I pitched it to Mack and he was sort of up for it but it seems he'd only be doing it for my sake and thinks I'd have a better time dancing with Rana without him there as the ball and chain. Christ, I'm so busy this week with the students' end of year show opening on Thursday and all my academic work, but it'll be good to get down to that LDN and have a breather, get some closure, see some pals. I haven't even thought about how I'm supposed to express my true me through DIY or everyday objects. I have some vague ideas about using dishcloths, steel wool scourers and a general kitchen sink vibe. Maybe I'll wear a plug chain as a necklace? I'm not going to give it too much thought.

Watching a live video I haven't seen before, I start to think that maybe most of this was about the music; the sexiness of it, the aspiration of being a performing musician, my desire to be the object of your (plural) desires as you play to an audience of me. I bet you're wondering why I set my sights on you particularly, Curt. To put it simply, I find you the most attractive. How shallow, eh? I think again of your lissome but goofy manner and how you drum and DJ and imagine us dancing as a warm-up to fucking. I can't really believe I'm going to see you on Saturday and I don't really know how or whether to prepare, or what my plan of action is, but I'll just have to drift along with whatever weird magnetism is pulling me towards you, towards *inner u*. Maybe this has all just been the universe's convoluted way of getting me to loosen up and party. If so, it's a bit of a piss-take.

Geraldine Snell

Saturday 20th May, 17:00

Rana's Flat: Manor House, London

At approximately 5pm, I make the journey northwards from Rose's in New Cross to Rana's near Manor House. I feel nauseous, jittery *and* heavy-hearted but know that I'll be put at ease by the next few hours catching up and getting ready with Rana. I'm slightly dazed as I take the orange line northwards, then westwards and the blue line north-eastwards for the last two stops. I walk to Rana's worrying that I don't have enough cash, worrying that the machines on this road will charge for me to withdraw money, worrying about what we will eat and drink, worrying that my now seldom used smoking tin with my tobacco and a bit of bud disappeared at some point during the coach ride down and I won't be able to smoke a joint in the early hours to soften the comedown, worrying that even if I did still have it the stuff makes me anxious anyway nowadays. I call R to ask if she needs me to get anything and to ask about the ATMs, trying to sound calm and carefree, and she puts me at ease, saying we'll sort it all out when I get to hers.

I arrive and dump my bag, greeted at the door by her warm, maternal embrace. We sit and catch up briefly over a brew before heading out to get cash from a free withdrawals ATM, bottles of gin, bitter lemon and tonic from a cheap offy, and takeaway jerk chicken from a reliable cafe. Rana asks about the writing so I tell her about it. She asks if it's like when you have a really intense dream about someone and feel like you know them – or that something very intimate has occurred between you, but you don't and it hasn't – and you have this overwhelming impulse to tell them and carry it on, but of course they don't really know what you're on about and think you're weird for dreaming about them. I tell her she's pretty much hit the nail on the head.

My appetite is non-existent but we set to work on the contents of our Styrofoam boxes, chewing the cud and putting the world to rights in our usual way. I feel stupid about the whole thing but I'm rationalising and neutralising the negative thoughts which threaten to cloud my mind and judgement telling myself: you

overlove

have every right to be there honey, you haven't done anything terrible boo, nothing awful's gonna happen sweetie, Rana doesn't hate you silly, in fact this whole thing has brought you two together for a much needed catch up and dance, so have a gin and bitter lemon mate, have a fag pal, put your slap on babe, forget it chuck.

After food and chatting we move into Rana's room and she puts Aretha on whilst we start getting ready. I watch the speed and skill she employs to accentuate her features out of the corner of my eye, seeing her gorgeous reflection in the mirror beaming flirtatiously when she clocks me looking admiringly her way, and I smile to myself as I dabble cluelessly with my cheap highlighter and contour kit. The atmosphere is one of contented anticipation, the sense that if for whatever reason we just decided to fuck it off and not go out, the getting ready and pre-drinking ritual will've been enough in itself anyway.

I sip my gin and bitter lemon and consider, out loud, whether to actually wear fake eyelashes or whether that's a step too far. We decide that I should do the rest of my makeup and eye makeup before judging whether the addition of fake eyelashes would be superfluous and try-hard. I coat my lips in dark pinkish red with the lippy Katy bought me in January and line them with a plumping liner I got free in a girly mag. I fill in my brows with darker powder than I ordinarily would because the lighting will be low and they'll need a bit of extra definition so as not to disappear in the dim light of the dancefloor. I unpin my hair from the shape I've scrunched it up in to lift the roots and further tousle its natural curls and scrunch my fingers through it to give it more volume, pinning the small front right section back off my face, leaving the longest bit hanging down, and tucking the shorter left bit behind my ear, on which I clip the small but dazzling diamante starfish cuff that I nicked from Claire's Accessories. I coat my eyes in a metallic pewter cream from a tiny tube which Mum gave me Christmases ago that just keeps giving after years of use, although it's slightly dried up and a bit flakes off onto the floor. I apply a subtly shimmering white-beige powder to the inner corner and area below the brow arch of each eye and work an iridescent, smokey grey shade into the outer crease of my eyelid, blending it with the metallic cream underneath. I line my top lids above the lashes with a fancy pen-style liner gifted to me as a thank you by my former boss Yvonne and I coat my lashes in some free mascara samples I've scavenged from Mack's mum's multi-buy makeup freebies, before I turn to Rana and ask her to evaluate the symmetry of my eyes, which she says need more darker tones extending further from my left eye towards the outer end of my brow.

I try on this navy sleeveless playsuit I bought years ago for a fiver in some high-street sale, but despite removing the bones from the torso section it still has an uncomfortable, deep-breath-suppressing corset feel. I know I'm gonna need my deep breaths tonight so I instead slip into my black bandage style cold shoulder V-neck crop-top and these amazing checked short shorts I foraged from Louise's hand-me-downs. Rana assures me that either outfit is tip-top, but I feel less inhibited and more 'me' in my own body in the top and shorts. I offer the same critical eye on the jacket she selects to wear over her black, plunging neckline dress and she settles on a stripy bolero that – in some ways – visually conjures the association of garden furniture or an apron, which we agree ticks the 'everyday' fancy dress theme box.

I spend too long faffing around with hooking a cheap plug onto the cheap plug-chain I bought from Wilko but eventually prise the metal open enough to hook it round my neck – which seems like a disaster waiting to happen – and I put on some plain black ankle socks under the balls of steel wool around my ankles so I can don kitchen sink adornment without enduring unnecessary abrasion.

At 9:30pm we agree to go over after half 10 because we know it'll be dead quiet early on, so I unearth the tarot deck Mack got me for my birthday and attempt to do a three card 'Situation, Action, Outcome' spread, even though all the YouTube videos we consult about how the heck to do a quick reading make it seem like you have to do a million practice runs and know the ins and outs of it all first. We perform it cynically over a fag and our gin and tonics (the bitter lemon ran out), but are both stunned when the 'situation' card we overturn is Four of Wands, which depicts "two female figures uplifting nosegays... at their side is a bridge over a moat leading to an old manorial house". We are STUNNED because we are two females in MANOR HOUSE about to attend a party in a former warehouse!!! The divinatory meanings of "country life, repose, concord, harmony, prosperity, peace and the perfected work of these" are less important, but depending on how you swing it could definitely relate to the situation and us – country bumpkins from up north – in our state of pre-party repose.

The action card is Six of Cups, which shows "children in an old garden, their cups filled with flowers" and suggests "reflecting on childhood, happiness, enjoyment, but coming rather from the past, things that have vanished" or "new relations, new environments and new knowledge" which is also eerie because we'd just been reminiscing about old friends and good times. Sure, the whole point of Tarot and mysticism is that you skew the interpretation to your situation so it always relates, but of all the cards, they still relate to a freaky degree. The outcome card is Queen of Wands, meaning "A dark woman or countrywoman, friendly, chaste, loving, honourable" and we feel we have to wait and see how the night pans out before evaluating its pertinence.

Time ticks by and we decide to just go for it with the fake eyelashes. My instinct tells me they're too much but I know I have to get over the shame and conflict I feel about the masque of femininity, so Rana expertly trims and applies them for me before we get on our dancing shoes – for her, chunky lace up boots; for me, my swag platform orthopaedic trainers – and depart the flat after taking a couple of giggly selfies together in front of the big mirror in the hallway. We walk, linked arm in arm, along the streets lined with houses and warehouses in the 11pm quiet, eased by the gin we've consumed, incredulous about the eerie accuracy of the tarot, and curious about what the evening will bring. Within ten minutes we find the portal to inner u – an inconspicuous industrial stairwell – and ascend the floors towards the music before reaching a glam but friendly duo on the door who tick our names off the list, stamp our hands with a distinctive Leela-designed logo, and tell us we're first here.

# #

We burst onto the empty dance floor, giggling to ourselves about being the first to arrive but comforted by the time this offers us to get our bearings and scout the place out. We ask the barman to take a picture of us together by some fairy lights before taking an exaggeratedly smiley picture of each other stood alone in the centre of the floor in front of the DJ booth, lit from behind by a grid of partially working light bulbs. Rana orders us gin and tonics whilst I read the bold text hung on plain white paper above; the sheets which say "U r a body of crystals", "Slip through ur own surface" and "Find your inner u" seem standard, benevolent dancefloor mantras but I am struck by the urgings of two in particular – "Use your mind as desire" and "Stay in the dream of the other" – which relate uncannily to my journey hitherto.

Because I'd set myself up for you rocking up late with pals or Leela – or not turning up at all – I am staggered when you are the next person to arrive, with a pixie-haired blonde lass who isn't Leela. My heart races when you shimmy in sooner than I thought you would, looking coolly over at Rana and I – the early arrivals, half-dancing by the bar – as you spin serenely in slow semi circles, your arms at 45 degrees like a slowed-down dandelion seed, as at ease on the dancefloor as you are at a drum-kit, and I pray that you don't recognise me from the Facebook add and message 199 days ago as I attempt to 'act natural', nonchalant, or normal at least.

I utter to Rana that it's you as we head upstairs to the mezzanine for a smoke. I relax into a low corner sofa and whilst we roll our cigs and chat, I see you and the blonde lass come up the stairs to sit down opposite but facing us at the other end of the seating area. You're in my sightline – sans jumper, arms buff in your trademark singlet – as I face Rana, and I stare at you across the room whilst I smoke, casually looking away when your eyes meet mine, somehow managing to maintain conversation about the furniture, the vibe, the tarot, despite the tingling butterflies sensation in my stomach, heart and groin.

People arrive in dribs and drabs but the dancefloor is still

overlove

mostly empty, and R and I join you and a few others for a bit of warm-up grooving as a friendly lass in a sequinned jumpsuit introduces herself. I subtly make eyes at you and am slightly dismayed that you avert yours sideways – connoting dismissal, evasion or perhaps possible attraction that's not indulged in due to relationship status – every time our gazes meet. I don't mind because you're at home with friends on the dancefloor and so am I, as I move and shake whilst scanning new faces in the room, fixating regularly back on the 'Use your mind as desire' sign above the DJ booth.

The club fills up and pretty soon Rana and I are in a rhythm of dancing, chatting, smoking, loo-breaking, drinking through to dancing again. I chat to new people, bonding with a girl from Bradford and a guy from Harrogate about the Yorkshire motherland and I dance dance dance – truly carefree – but you're on my radar Curt, and the pressure to speak to you – to say something: AnYtHiNg – weighs down on me.

The dancefloor is small so without necessarily intending to, I end up near you a few times. I'm sure I detect an earthy odour you as you slip lithely through a gap between me and the person next to me, and I catch myself flaring my nostrils to breathe you in, a little like Hannibal or Edward Cullen. I am sure also – beyond reasonable doubt, or surer at least than I was about the eye contact at the gig in November – that your hand or arm absolutely accidentally grazes my bum as you move around the dancefloor, darting content but restless between friends. It definitely happened because Rana clocks it too: I'm thinking it was maybe that universal magnetism I've been banging on about, moving my bum at the exact moment your arm moved through the gap.

Around half 1 Rana approaches me with a pill she sourced from a shifty guy on the mezzanine, and whilst we never intended to get 'on it' on it, we split the pill and say cheers to us, tenderly gushing about how wonderful it is to get to do this together and how handy it is that we found a party we don't even have to sort transport back from. It gives me the juice I need to keep dancing and I come up on a subtle high, slightly accelerated and enhanced in my meanderings from dancefloor to mezz to loo to barside water top-up to dancefloor, all the time gazing at you through the soft framing of dancing bodies.

At one point I see Sophie who actually published my adolescent crush sonnets in a zine called 'Tits or GTFO' a few years ago! Another strange coincidence, I think to myself as I consider the synchronicity of my crush trajectory with the inner u vibe. Our chatting makes me feel silly about my feeling that I have no right to be here, that this isn't my scene, even if this type of party – this place where Guardian journalists, professional musicians, white guys that work in the middle East and speak fluent Arabic, women that run ethical clothing brands, artists, kinksters, and cosmopolitan people freely coexist – is worlds away from my typical Saturday night.

It is soon after this, after much mingling, dancing and generally floating about, that I begin to feel restless and weighed down by the confession I'm desperate to make to you. The opportunity presents itself when I'm stood by the bar, and you stop dancing with some lass who isn't Leela or the blonde lass and seem to be hovering on the periphery of the dance floor in a sort of limbo state. Necessity grips me and I sidle over to you, tap you on your warm, bare arm and say:

Can I chat to you a minute?

apprehensively, respectfully, flirtatiously, looking coyly up at you through the stupid fuckin eyelashes as you lean in and reply:

Go for it

looking neither confused or bemused or like anything at all, of course, and the music's quite loud so I lean further up towards your right ear and you're not as tall as I thought you'd be but maybe it's just cos I've got my platforms on and I'm up on the pill and I say:

I have a silly crush on you and I'm kind of writing about it, and I just wanted to tell you, really

overlove

in my quiet, mumbly manner; you interrupt with some *what?*'s or *pardon?*'s in between so I say it louder so you can hear it over the music before you ask:

Oh, what kind of writing?
or *in what sense?*
and definitely *what's the form of it?*

which pleases me even if you're just being polite and I say:

It's kind of a diary love letter

A diary what?

you can't hear over the music

love letter

and you are kind of flirty and leaning in or at least not leaning away and I think you are maybe flattered but also totally indifferent or processing what I've just said and I kick myself I SHOULDN'T HAVE WORN THESE FUCKIN FAKE EYELASHES, IT LOOKS SO DESPERATE, IDIOT!! but I also feel totally natural and right and comfortable in your presence and you're as charismatic as I thought, you smell woody and earthy like sex in a good way, and then I continue:

so I've like, pushed it, aped it

realising that was maybe the wrong verb, confirmed when you say:

You've what it?

and I clarify:

like... magnified it, stretched it out
made it significant for the purpose of the literature

but not so articulately, and I carry on:

Geraldine Snell

Like, obviously it's not really about you
per se, and
I'm in a relationship and stuff, but, meh, this is all cool

and I dismissively hand gesture as you affirm :

yeah, of course, all literature is about the person who writes it

and your voice is melodic and gentle, your manner cool and serene, your eye contact as distant and ambivalent as it was in the beach dream I had three months earlier and I wonder how to spin it out or what to propose because I have no plan of action, I'm just stood here fluttering my fake eyelashes expecting you to read my mind and complete my fantasy, suddenly aware that I've just waded in with a pretty intense introduction so I try to lighten the tone, saying:

I had this vision of telling you, and you forgetting,
and then waking up and remembering and being like, what the fuck?

Yeah…

and I sense some indifference before you go full drummer boy and use me as some audience litmus test to gauge the vibe, saying:

I feel like the music was like, up here,
and now it's down here a bit,
and it needs to go up again

whilst doing some oscillating wavy shape with your buff but lithe drummer boy arms like a valley side down then up and maybe you're just using a metaphor to hint that I've just taken the whole vibe down a notch for you but I don't think so I think you just wanted to change tack rather than discuss me and my desire any further, understandably, but in any case I mirror your wavy arm gesture without meaning to, propelled by some strange magnetism because that's what this lustLOVElimerence

overlove

DOES – we are but puppets on a predetermined biological programming string – and after a silent but-not-in-an-awkward-way moment you slope off without comment but without being rude either and it's all quite ok although it's slowly dawning on me that whilst what I really want is for us to dance and kiss and fuck, whilst what I really want is for you to look into my soul and mirror it back to me more than you just did, I guess now isn't the time or place and I guess you're not so inclined and I guess maybe it's a strange, random and totally insignificant thing for you and you're here with your friends and have this whole life and you don't know me and I don't know you and whatever happened happened in my head and isn't real.

I keep dancing on the inner u euphoria and I tell Rana I've told you and she tells me she's proud of me and we take a short video and a dark, dark selfie in the glow of the fairy lights and I am up on the pill, elated, somewhere deep down deeply let down but for the time being I'm soaring, I own the world, I have exorcised something, exorcised the shame associated with my desire, and things come flooding back like the time, aged 17, I said I wanted to mount this geek called Josh and sent him a letter and everyone took the piss and someone said he burned the letter, and in this moment at inner u it's all gone, partially lifted and my true me has been exposed and I've done it, I'm so glad I've done it, I've spoken to you and you've acknowledged, you know and you saw me, YOU SEE ME!!, my true me, being seen and recognised for what for who I am was some real deep shit, some real baby crying out and no one coming yet still crying out for connection, momentarily sated by a warm embrace or meeting of the eyes which I'm still high from so I carry on

trying to make eyes, they meet occasionally and you avert and I think I SHOULD STARE MORE CONFidENTLY but I don't want to be invasive or predatory and in any case, I'm there to dance with my gal pal, to dance alone, to dance the night away which I damn well do and it's so wonderful and liberating to bounce around in my body of crystals, to find my inner u, to slip through my own surface after all this using my mind as desire, all this staying in the dream of the other before

I begin to get the familiar grief feeling ripping ripping ripping through my chest and soul because whilst I'm dancing high but all alone on the dancefloor some guy from earlier who liked that I was from Yorkshire starts edging towards me and I can feel his stares and see him in my peripheral vision and I deliberately turn away avoiding all eye contact, looking up the stairs, hoping Rana would come down and save me, half thinking I should go and dance with you, beg you to pretend that you're my boyfriend and save save SAVE me from this guy I'm not into but you're not interested, Curt, you're not bothered and that combined with this hovering guy takes me right down from my total empowerment buzz and into a deep deep reserved grief feeling and I depart the dancefloor, numbly ascend the stairs up to the mezzanine where Rana is chatting with friendly Tom, and sit down on a comfy leather chair, broken inside and seething that despite enjoying being all alone on the dancefloor, despite being in my element, I couldn't bear to dance to the end of the last song because I had to slip away from this guy who then followed me up the stairs, and he comes and sits on the chair next to me as I roll a fag and keeps staring, I feel the weight of his gaze, buckling under it inside but maintaining a steely disinterested veneer on the outside and he starts saying something quietly so I ignore him, pretend not to hear and he says 'hey' louder and something about being sorry for not introducing himself earlier and he tells me his name is Dave and I don't look at him whilst I say "Hi Dave" but I deliberately don't reciprocate in this name exchange and I so want it to be you coming and joining me and staring me down and undressing me with your eyes but it's not, it's this dude who has no radar and doesn't read my FUCK OFF I JUST WANTED TO DANCE TO THE LAST GODDAMN SONG ALONE OR WITH MY GAL signals and I keep looking at Rana trying to make eye contact with her and manage, eventually, to hint through a widening of the eyes and a sideways tilt in Dave's direction that I'm uncomfortable and she comes and sits next to me and it occurs to me that the

overlove

cool kids – that you – are leaving

but Rana hugs me and after having a few tokes on friendly Tom's joint I sink into the chair, melded into her arms and bosom and eventually we make a move, uttering such things as "what a beautiful evening" and "we found our inner u" and she says "I really respect what you're doing, you fuckin did it, you told him, you did all you could, you've done it, what a wonderful evening"

and we walk out, her hand around my waist propping me up, down the road in the sublime glow of the pink sunrise which blends into blue with a perfect crescent of silver and it's so quiet and all the partygoers have utter respect for the serenity of this post-party moment, except the dickwad that throws his bottle into some garden which loudly smashes – WHAT A DICK! – it's astoundingly beautiful and we gravitate towards these blue bunkers, passing them slowly, walking back to Rana's where she gets in bed and I

sit on the floor, coming down, as terrible grief feelings swirl with expansive spiritually contented feelings as the illusion is finally shattered my bubble is completely burst and I feel so broken broken broken sick broken hearted but still somehow high and I hope I'll dream of you and forget the fact that nothing happened and then remember it in the morning, like remember I said you'd forget and then remember in the morning? but I guess I'm forgetting that you probably won't even think twice about it because the whole exchange to you was as insignificant, inconsequential or NOn-EXIstenT as those glances I'd hoped we'd shared at that gig 199 days ago and all this overloving was for nothing, bar the deepening of my life-love-GrieF, the pushing of this impulse to heighten life to art; as nobly foolish as the nightingale piercing itself on the thorn of the white rose to turn it red for the sake of love with the blood of its pure, willing heart.

Sunday 21st May, 06:00

Rana's Flat: Manor House, London

I'm too high and low to sleep and dunno what to do with myself but scribble down the beginning of the end of whatever this literary abomination is in my notebook. I'm so keyed up that my hands can't write the way they usually can and I look down at the 4 pages of punctuationless, raw scrawling I've just secreted and decide, in my 6am delirium, to send it to you because I'm overwhelmed by the femaleness of this endeavour and the potency of the image of the open notebook in my naked lap, like a baby I've just squeezed out, and for some reason feel the need to follow up – even though your response just a few hours earlier was pretty much an extended shrug – just in case you didn't grasp the magnitude of it from my calm confession to you. I send a photograph of the book rested on my bare crotch with the text:

06:13
I have just given birth to the ending of my c10,000 word crush diary love letter to you! It will all be edited and refined now. I will send it you when it's done, if you want. Or not if you're creeped out. I'd want to read it if someone used me as a vehicle for self-transformation and creative exploration though! Thank you muse, and thanks for leading me to inner u
I truly legit found my inner u tonight xx 👀🕯️💨❤️☺️

and another image of me naked in the mirror, my 'lady garden' concealed by my notebook along with the message:

06:37
Unless of course you want the story to continue… like, in a casual way, I have a primary partner.
Og sorry I will shut up now I'm just rly high n this has been building for a whiiiile zzz

I'm feeling beyond the point of shame or embarrassment but

overlove

have a sense somewhere deep in my saner self that this is weird and sort of harassing behaviour. My desire to exhibit myself and my literary catharsis is clearly greater than any of these concerns. I don't really sleep and spend the Sunday going for Turkish brunch with Rana, where she and I talk about how as a guy you probably think nothing of the fact that someone's obsessed with you because you probably think "yeah, why wouldn't she be?" but that if it was us we just wouldn't believe someone could fancy us that much.

Later on I meet Molly and Jamie for a walk in the sun before Wetherspoons and I somehow manage to function and converse, slightly asleep at the wheel but on ok form nonetheless, despite the strange sensations of love and grief that bounce off the walls of my human shell and the mixed feeling that whilst some huge weight has been lifted and I am now as light as a feather, an unpleasantly familiar and more acute heaviness has come to replace it and weigh me down. Although on the surface I have a great time talking with Molly and Jamie – who seem intrigued by the writing and ask "aren't you in a relationship though?" before we talk about monogamy and being in love with the idea of love – and we have a true laugh as well as deep conversation like true friends do the whole afternoon and early evening, I'm slyly scanning Finsbury and Clissold Parks, the streets of Stoke Newington, and the pavements of Manor House for you, Curt.

Geraldine Snell

Monday 22nd May, 16:00

Skipton Train: Leeds, Yorkshire

On the train back from that London, I receive your response. Isn't it strange how I was on the train the first time you messaged, and I'm on the train now? Imagine if I'm in the same carriage! I'm exhilarated but apprehensive as I open it and read:

16:17
I'm not sure entirely what to say, but I suppose it might be an interesting read..regarding your second offer, thats very flattering, but i'm currently in a primary partner sort of situation and that's plenty to keep me busy just now. have an excellent week x

and for some reason, although your response again doesn't invite any sort of response, although it is very decent and I tingle with satisfaction that you've replied at all and disappointment that you don't wanna know and it's another closed response, I also think kudos to you, Curt, and feel the need to apologise and justify and backtrack on my whole inappropriate nude pic stuff and I spend longer than I realise composing a longer than intended message in which I try to sound as sane and rational as possible, like this has all been an intellectual exercise, and over twenty minutes later – worried that you might've seen the "…" animation for a solid twenty minutes and wondered what the fuck else I have to say to you or bother you with, I message:

16:41
no I shouldn't have made that second offer I was just high on drugs and dancing and writing and glancing and thought 'yolo go big or go home' kinda thing, it was juvenile. I gathered you were in a relationship (not through any actual stalking, btw, your illustration led me there. Indeed everyone has so much online now, one of my students did a project based on a woman's YouTube videos about her whole family and traced it back six generations just through googlin) but yeah I was quite enthralled to find that mental health and female gaze interests intersect in who I presume is your partner and if, in the

overlove

> *unlikely (but maybe not, given current trends, and NO its nothing like I love dick altho was, of course, inspired by that) event that this thang got published I want to commission some illustrations but that's a different conversation for a future time when I have knitted the fragments into decent literature etc etc etc you have an excellent week too thanks for replying that's very decent and hope you don't feel impinged on/ violated it's a benign and positive thing that won't read so solipsistically ultimately (that's the plan) I'll shh now x*

and Mack tells me I need to remember that you don't know me and that I need to be careful because you could see it as harassment and I tell him, if you were that bothered you'd have declined my friend request, if you were that bothered you'd have blocked me on messenger, if you were that bothered you would change your privacy settings to prevent any old randomer messaging or liking or commenting on your posts or accessing your personal page from the Google top result. Mack concurs: you are truly indifferent.

Geraldine Snell

Monday 29th May, 16:40

Home: Oakworth, Yorkshire

Curt, I'm feeling really resentful towards you for not reciprocating which proves how true it is that we need to be responsible for our own emotions, how true it is that much of our upset comes from our own projections and insecurities rather than others' actions. Unless they actually act badly, obviously...

I keep imagining you in my day-to-day; I see you stood at the foot of my bed gazing wistfully out of the window after sex, or washing up after I've cooked us a meal. I imagine you round at mine in a mood, or deep in thought, but that being ok. I imagine you experiencing a visceral and perhaps involuntary prickle of exhilaration - maybe even a stirring in the loins - upon opening my pictures and messages, and feel a grim sense of satisfaction that despite not knowing you, I may have affected you in some small way. I imagine receiving an early harassment notice from the police, and sort of desire this as recognition that I have in some way influenced your actions, which I almost crave as it would indicate greater reciprocation of feeling – even if that feeling is negative – than your apparent ambivalence.

I guess you could've been anyone. You are a version of the same thing I've been falling for my whole life: the Hollywood hunk, the hot teacher, the chavvy guy at school; the cute postman or plumber, the cheeky barman, or the more attractive co-worker of the bunch; you are any of the people I've latched onto and will continue to latch onto at school or work or on the train; you are 'what I go to school for'; you are the distant Other I seek, even when I've found a near and pretty much perfect other in Mack. I suppose at 25, in the midst of mood volatility and figuring out how to be a person, focusing on you was more tangible than any of the above, due in part to the fact that I found you and you were closer, more accessible, than I thought you'd be.

overlove

Wednesday 31st May, 20:20

Home: Oakworth, Yorkshire

Writing right now reminds me of the excitement and adrenaline that was coursing through my blood when writing after inner u. I'm still pettily plaintive like a typical love's fool but it's a week where I'd rather do my writing than come to your gig; it never leaves me high and dry like you do, Curt. Lol, only kidding, I said that for dramatic effect. I know that it'd have been way weirder and nigh-on-ridiculous if you'd actually gone for it, and that given that you don't know me or didn't consent to any of this, you owe me nothing.
Still…

In the parallel universe of my masochistic mind, my arm brushes against yours, I bask in your keen and lust-struck gaze and our bodily proximity makes us both twitch with arousal.

In the sticky projector reel of my imagination, I dance with my arse in your crotch and you look as engrossed as you did in the vid where I slowed your drumming to a quarter of the speed and watched it on a loop whilst I brought myself to orgasm six times in a row.

In my stuck-record reveries, I consensually nip through the cat-flap of the walled garden to occasionally experience the warm, complete falling feeling – and hopefully just plain old friendship too – that comes from a reciprocated infatuation with a more distant magical Other.

Sunday 4th June, 09:30

Mack's House: Bingley, Yorkshire

Shit, that was meant to be the end but I just woke from three dumb dreams, the last of which involved me watching you play a solo drum set live in a hot, packed and dimly lit venue where afterwards - stood by the bar - you toppled, fell and hit your head, which began bleeding out all over the floor. I ran to you, attempting to reassure you that help was on its way, saying "stay with me, Curt, it's all ok", inwardly panicking as I fumbled for something to absorb the blood or stem the deep red flow, which leaked out at a worrying rate as you waned before me. I urged you to stay conscious, but I woke before the whole life/death situation resolved itself, somewhat disturbed but actually slightly thankful to my brain for killing you off, so to speak.

overlove

Monday 19th June, 15:30

Top North Guest House: Chiang Mai, Thailand

Ok, I didn't want to get into footnotes and further dialogues with myself over time. This is just a little one because I'm out on 'holiday' editing this mess and don't want to merely erase 13th January's self-dismissal, but instead to contradict the ridiculous statement I made from my wizened perspective 5 months later. Why the heck am I so apologetic, so dismissive of my contribution to literature that I've described it as 'tired ground'?!?! How is this tired ground? Fuck the novel: lay it bare. THE FEMALE GAZE IS JUST RAMPING UP, M888

Geraldine Snell

Wednesday 14th February, 21:10

Mack's House: Bingley, Yorkshire

A quick update Curt: I pretty much nipped this all in the bud last May and focused on the art of it rather than the life of it, but I've still had many dreams about you and have continued to keep a distant eye on you online. In terms of the art of it I edited and refined the writing, titled it *overlove*, fleshed some bits out and trimmed down others, and set about developing an episodic and likely online film work. I found a small but cool independent publisher called Dostoyevsky Wannabe who are gonna put it out in October and it'll have an ISBN and you'll be able to buy for like, a fiver, online! I'm gonna bite the bullet and enquire about commissioning an illustration from Leela, although I've seriously questioned my simplistic, heteronormative assumptions about your relationship, particularly as she seems to be living in Berlin.

I've been half-living in London since September through a few serendipitous twists of fate involving friends and an anomalously cheap room which happens to be situated about ten minutes' walk from you in Seven Sisters, which I know because you still post really revealing shit on your public Facebook, like that recent callout for a sublet in your warehouse conversion which includes pictures of its interior, or the picture of records delivered to you in a pizza box which had your actual full phone number and address on. Given that we also now share a mutual friend – this ace person who runs a reading group which facebook's algorithms, or that universal magnetism again, clearly wanted me to attend as it kept cropping on my feed due a pal being 'interested' in it – I can see even more of your profile, from events you say you're interested in or going to attend to pictures going back to goofy braces-era 2007, and even a recent post by the DJ lady who shared a sweet video of you skating on the street outside 'the house' on Facebook, which corroborated the information about where you live, given the distinctive art on the buildings visible behind your slowed, gliding form.

You're on tour again, supporting a stadium-level artiste and I found myself wondering the other day if you get nervous when playing an arena? Paula texted me on Friday night saying she was watching you live and thought of me, and I told her to blow you a kiss from me. I also only twigged the other day that it was really weird for me to tell you I'd written about you rather than just trying to flirt with you, and it confirmed my suspicion that this was never even about sex. It also occurred to me that maybe I'm not the only 'mad bitch' fan girl you've had contact or find you, although I'm surely the best(worst) given that I've written a 20,000 word epic about it?

Besides all that I've made significant artistic, professional and personal progress, Macky's still my no.1 boi and I'm getting a proposal together for a book which starts with a gantt chart mapping out a lifetime of crushes and romances. Your bar is actually pretty small on that chart, even if its colour density signifies great intensity.. So happy Valentine's Day again Curt <3 I hope you find it to be "an interesting read" but I also don't care whether you read it or not because I know now that it truly was never about you xx

The End

ACKNOWLEDGEMENTS

Sunday 29th July, 20:56

Centre Pompadour: Picardie, France

I have just finished the final draft, aided in my editing by a bunch of incredible friends and artists whose supportive *and* critical comments helped me to shape a text I was often much too close to: thanks a trillion Daisy Lafarge, Sian Robinson Davies, Katy White, Molly Palmer, Genevieve Giuffre, Declan Middleton, Raghad Bezizi, Daisy Dooks, Harry Meadley, Kirsty Roxburgh and Clare Walker. Thank you Mum, Dad, Ants and the rest of the family for supporting me and my artistic endeavours despite it not being a route taken by any of your friends or family - apart from Great Uncle Paul (Rutherford) who sadly suffered for his music - although I really hope you're not reading this though because that means you've read the book which I'd rather you hadn't, HA. Thank you Nan for inspiring my artistic proclivities with postcards, quotes, books and gallery visits from birth, pretty much. Thank you to 'Mack' for being my partner this last 8 and a half years and always considering my feelings first even if they've been destructive or difficult at times, and for absolutely ALWAYS taking the piss out of me. Thanks again a trillion times to Daisy Lafarge for being my contextual reference point genie and kindred spirit sister and offering support in an irrational and mythic, as well as critical, intellectual sense. Thanks to 'Rana' for humouring and supporting me in my attendance of 'inner u' and being a warm and judgementless bezzie in general. Thanks to 'Leela' and the creators of inner u for the visual inspiration and slogans which synced so incredibly well with *overlove*. Thanks to Nicky Green for letting me be her life coach training guinea pig when I moved home after uni and helping me sort my life out. Thanks to Conch.fyi, Philomena Epps at Orlando Zine, Michaela Spiegel at Centre Pompadour. And finally Richard and Vikki aka Dostoyevsky Wannabe for existing publishing *overlove* and other such underground 'unsolicited' unagented unadulterated stuff, and to Vikki again for designing the cover I envisaged ('Leela' never replied about doing a cover illustration and I don't blame her because the email I sent her was more ridiculous, full on and incoherent than this list of acknowledgements.)

REFERENCES

Easton, D. & Hardy, J. (2009) The Ethical Slut: A Practical Guide to Polyamory, Open Relationships & Other Adventures. 2nd ed. Celestial Arts: Berkeley

Fisher, M. (2009) Capitalist Realism: Is There No Alternative? Zero: Ropley

Hollis, J, (1998) The Eden Project: In Search of the Magical Other - Jungian Perspective on Relationship. Inner City Books: Toronto

Irigaray, L. &Marder, M. (2016) Through Vegetal Being: Two Philosophical Perspectives. Columbia University Press: New York

Kraus, C. (1997) I Love Dick. Semiotexte: Los Angeles

Geraldine Snell (b.1992, Keighley) is an artist, writer and musician based between London - where she is completing a masters at the Slade - and her native West Yorkshire where she teaches Fine Art. overlove is her debut publication and you can find more of her work – including some kind of video adaptation of overlove- online at geraldinesnell.com and @geraldinesnell.

Still taken from *overlove* video by Geraldine Snell

Still taken from *overlove* video by Geraldine Snell

Still taken from *overlove* video by Geraldine Snell

More from Dostoyevsky Wannabe, 2018

DOSTOYEVSKY WANNABE ORIGINALS

Honest Days by Matt Bookin
The Peeler by Bertie Marshall
Lou Ham: RAS by Paul Hawkins
A Hypocritical Reader by Rosie Šnajdr
Dark Hour by Nadia de Vries
Yeezus in Furs by Shane Jesse Christmass

DOSTOYEVSKY WANNABE SAMPLERS

Cassette 85 Guest-Edited by Troy James Weaver

DOSTOYEVSKY WANNABE CITIES

Bristol Guest-Edited by Paul Hawkins

DOSTOYEVSKY WANNABE EXPERIMENTAL

Metempoiesis by Rose Knapp
Liberating the Canon Guest-Edited by Isabel Waidner
Sovereign Invalid by Alan Cunningham
Blooming Insanity by Chuck Harp
Girl at End by Richard Brammer

DOSTOYEVSKY WANNABE X

Poem, A Chapbook by Timmy Reed
The Rink by Aaron Kent

Dostoyevsky Wannabe

Printed in Poland
by Amazon Fulfillment
Poland Sp. z o.o., Wrocław